WOODRIDGE PUBLIC LIBRARY
W9-ATT-584

Raising the Flag

by Anastasia Suen
illustrated by Jeff Ebbeler

Content Consultant:
Vicki F. Panaccione, Ph.D.
Licensed Child Psychologist
Founder, Better Parenting Institute

visit us at
www.abdopublishing.com

Published by Magic Wagon, a division of the ABDO Publishing Group, 8000 West 78th Street, Edina, Minnesota, 55439.

Printed in the United States.

Text by Anastasia Suen
Illustrations by Jeff Ebbeler
Edited by Patricia Stockland
Interior layout and design by Becky Daum
Cover design by Becky Daum

Library of Congress Cataloging-in-Publication Data

Suen, Anastasia.
Raising the flag / Anastasia Suen ; illustrated by Jeffery Ebbeler.
p. cm. — (Main Street school)
Summary: Omar shows Megan and Latasha how to take care of the school's flag when they have flag duty.
ISBN-13: 978-1-60270-031-4
[1. Flags—Fiction. 2. Patriotism—Fiction. 3. Schools—Fiction.] I. Ebbeler, Jeffrey, ill. II. Title.
PZ7.S94343Raf 2007
[E]—dc22

2007004693

Latasha walked into the office. "It's my week to help with the flag," she said proudly to the lady in the office.

"Aren't you the lucky one!" said the lady. She put a check next to Latasha's name.

"There you are," said Megan. "We were waiting for you."

"Let's go," said Omar. He held the flag. It was folded into a small triangle.

"Have you ever done this before?" asked Latasha.

"I've gotten to do this lots of times," replied Omar. "I'm a Cub Scout."

"This will be my first time," said Latasha.

"Me, too!" said Megan.

"It's not hard," said Omar. "I'll hold the flag while you unfold it. Make sure it doesn't touch the ground."

"Why?" asked Latasha.

"Because it stands for our country," answered Omar.

"I'll untuck the end," said Omar. He pulled the edge of the flag out of the fold.

"Now it's your turn," said Omar. "Unfold the flag."

Latasha and Megan unfolded the flag. "Look at all the stars!" said Latasha.

"And here are the stripes!" said Megan. "It's so cool to see the flag up close."

"The 50 stars stand for the 50 states. The 13 stripes stand for the 13 original colonies," said Omar.

"I didn't know that!" exclaimed Megan. "Now what do we do?"

"Now open it the other way," said Omar.

Latasha and Megan carefully unfolded the flag, once, twice.

"Now we can raise it," said Omar.

Megan reached over to the pole and grabbed a hook.

"I'll start," said Megan, and she put a hook in the hole by the stripes.

"Wait!" said Omar. "That's the top hook."

"So?" asked Megan.

"The stars are on the top," said Latasha.

"Oh," said Megan. She took out the hook.

"Give that hook to Latasha," said Omar.

Megan handed the top hook to Latasha. Latasha put the hook in the hole by the stars. The flag hung from the rope.

"One more hook and we're done," said Omar.

"I'll do it," said Latasha.

She put the hook in the hole by
the stripes.

"I'll pull the rope," said Omar.
Latasha watched as the flag rose
to the top of the pole.

It looks beautiful! thought Latasha.

Screech, beep!

Latasha turned around. It was already time
for morning assembly!

Miss K's class was standing in line.

But we get to stay here by the flag, thought Latasha.

"Good morning," said the principal into the microphone.

"Good morning," replied the children at Main Street School.

"Let's begin with the pledge," said the principal.

Latasha turned to face the flag. She put her hand over her heart.

"I pledge allegiance to the flag of the United States of America...."

Latasha glanced over at Megan.

"And to the republic for which it stands..."

What was Megan doing?

"One nation under God...."

Why wasn't Megan saying the pledge?

"Indivisible..."

Why was Megan looking at her nails?

"...with liberty and justice for all."

"Megan," whispered Latasha.

Megan turned around.

"And now we will sing 'God Bless America'," said the principal.

Megan rolled her eyes.

Megan turned back around as the music started.

What is that all about? wondered Latasha. *I love this song!*

The music played over the loudspeaker. All of the children at Main Street School sang together, all except Megan.

PRINCIPAL

After the song, it was time for announcements.

The principal said, "I'd like to thank Latasha, Megan, and Omar for caring for our flag this week. It's a very important job."

Everyone looked at Latasha, Megan, and Omar.

Latasha smiled. *It is a very important job.*

We even get out of class early, thought Latasha. *We have to take down the flag before school gets out.*

"Have a wonderful day," said the principal.

The lines of teachers and students went to class one by one.

"Are you okay?" asked Latasha.

"Sure," said Megan, "why?"

"You didn't salute the flag," said Latasha, "or say the pledge or sing."

"That's boring," said Megan. "We do it every day."

"Don't you care about your country?" asked Latasha.

"What?" asked Megan.

Latasha replied, "My dad told me you show you care about the country by how you treat the flag."

"I didn't know that," said Megan. She put her hand over her heart and looked at the flag.

"I *do* care about my country!"

What Do You Think?

1. Why do Latasha, Megan, and Omar raise a flag in front of the school?
2. Why do they say the Pledge of Allegiance at school every day?
3. Why did everyone in the school sing "God Bless America"?
4. Why is it important to hang the flag?

Words to Know

allegiance—loyal support for someone or something.
indivisible—not able to be divided or broken into pieces.
justice—fair and impartial behavior or treatment.
liberty—freedom.
pledge—to make a sincere promise.

Fun Facts

Do you know how to fold a flag?

1. Fold the stripes up over the stars.
2. Fold the flag in half again so the stars show.
3. Fold the bottom striped corner up to make a triangle.
4. Fold that triangle in toward the stars.
5. Keep folding until you reach the end of the stars.
6. Tuck in the last edge of the stars.

Miss K's Classroom Rules

1. Say the Pledge of Allegiance.
2. Sing "God Bless America."
3. Show respect to the flag.

Web Sites

To learn more about patriotism, visit ABDO Publishing Company on the World Wide Web at **www.abdopublishing.com**. Web sites about patriotism are featured on our Book Links page. These links are routinely monitored and updated to provide the most current information available.